Mama's Business Trip
Bunny's Staycation

Lori Richmond

SCHOLASTIC INC.

FOR MATTHEW,

A JET-SETTING, CAMERA-TOTING PAPA WHO PITCHES TENTS
IN THE LIVING ROOM AND CRAFTS TRAINS OUT OF FOAM CORE;

AND FOR MAMAS EVERYWHERE

ISBN 978-1-338-28092-0 • 10 9 8 7 6 5 4 3 2 1   18 19 20 21 22 • Printed in the U.S.A. 08 • First printing 2018
The art was created in ink and watercolor, and composited digitally. No bunnies were harmed in the making of this book.
The text was set in 20 pt. Kepler Std Medium and Kepler Std Medium Italic. The display type was set in Kepler Std Caption.
Art direction by Marijka Kostiw. Book design by Lori Richmond and Marijka Kostiw

Mama is going away
on a business trip . . .

and Bunny doesn't like it one bit.

Mama won't be here for bedtime stories tonight, thought Bunny.

But if I make
the suitcase go away,
Mama can't leave!

Then Bunny has
an even *better* idea . . .

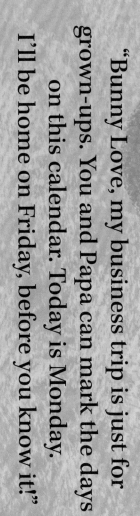

"Bunny Love, my business trip is just for grown-ups. You and Papa can mark the days on this calendar. Today is Monday. I'll be home on Friday, before you know it!"

That night, Bunny sniffles all the way through bedtime stories.

"Papa, I wish we could go somewhere little bunnies can go, too."

"Let's do it," said Papa. "We'll leave in the morning."

The next day,
Bunny and Papa
wake up early . . .

get the car ready . . .

and set off
on a grand adventure.

On Tuesday, a trip to the tropics . . .

On Wednesday, a wintry wonderland . . .

And on Thursday, a safari adventure!

But sometimes even the bravest adventurer misses Mama.

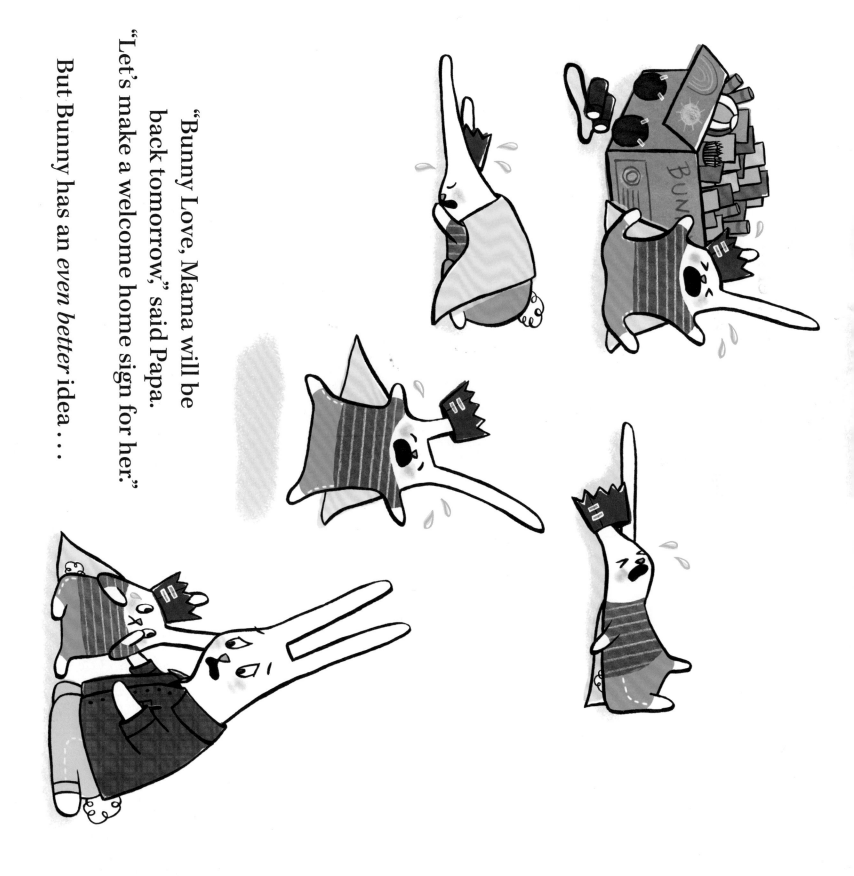

"Bunny Love, Mama will be back tomorrow," said Papa. "Let's make a welcome home sign for her."

But Bunny has an *even better* idea . . .

for one more
very special adventure.

On Friday, Mama is home at last.

"Hurry — come inside!" said Bunny.

SURPRISE!

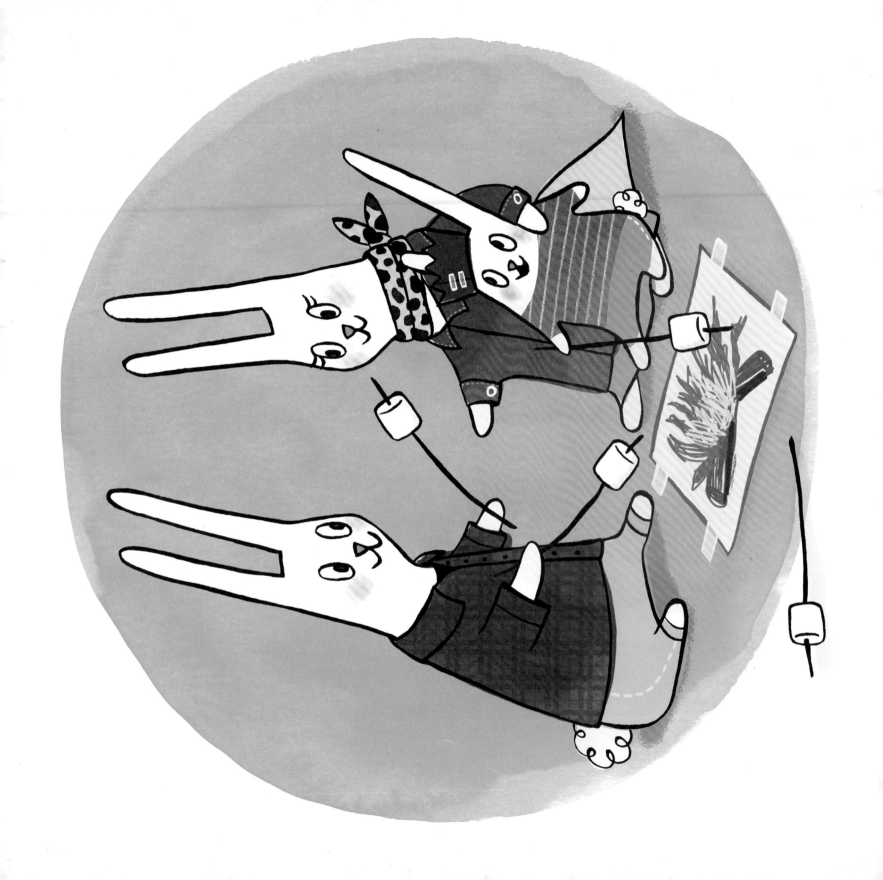